THE KATIE LYNN COOKIE COMPANY

PRESIDENT: KATIE LYNN
VICE PRESIDENT: TINA
HEAD BAKER: GRANDMA

AGENDA:

1. TO KEEP MAKING SUPER-SCRUMPTIOUS-YUMMY-DELICIOUS COOKIES!

2. TO FIND A NEW COOKIE THAT EVERYONE WILL GO APE FOR (AND RAISE MONEY FOR THE APE HOUSE AT THE ZOO)!

3. TO KEEP TINA'S LITTLE BROTHER OUT OF THE WAY LONG ENOUGH TO GET THE NEW COOKIES READY IN TIME FOR THE ZOO BENEFIT!

4. TO KEEP MOM'S FRENCH COOKING OUT OF THE KITCHEN—AND HER FROGS' LEGS OUT OF THE COOKIE DOUGH!

5. TO HELP JONATHAN NEXT DOOR LOOK FOR HIS MISSING PET FROG...IT MUST BE AROUND SOMEWHERE.

*To Shana, for taking over the reins so expertly—
and to
Gwen, Charles, James, and Tambye,
with all my love!*

Text copyright © 2000 by G. E. Stanley.
Illustrations copyright © 2000 by Linda Dockey Graves.
All rights reserved under International and Pan-American Copyright
Conventions. Published in the United States of America by Random House,
Inc., New York, and simultaneously in Canada by Random House of Canada
Limited, Toronto.

www.randomhouse.com/kids

Library of Congress Cataloging-in-Publication Data
Stanley, George Edward.
Frogs' legs for dinner? / by G. E. Stanley ;
illustrated by Linda Dockey Graves.
p. cm. — (The Katie Lynn Cookie Company; #2)
"A Stepping Stone Book."
Summary: Mrs. Cooke's new enthusiasm for French cooking creates chaos
in the kitchen and endangers Katie Lynn's cookie-baking business.
ISBN 0-679-89221-4 (trade). — ISBN 0-679-99221-9 (lib. bdg.)
[1. Cookery—Fiction]
I. Graves, Linda Dockey, ill. II. Title.
PZ7.S78694Fr 2000 [Fic]—dc21 98-47052

Printed in the United States of America April 2000 10 9 8 7 6 5 4 3 2 1

The Katie Lynn Cookie Company

#2

Frogs' Legs for Dinner?

by G. E. Stanley

illustrated by Linda Dockey Graves

A STEPPING STONE BOOK™
Random House 🏠 New York

Frogs' Legs
for Dinner?

Contents

Chapter One

Flying Pies

"Sit down, everyone!" said Mrs. Cooke. "Dinner's ready!"

Katie Lynn and her best friend, Tina, joined Mr. Cooke and Grandma at the kitchen table.

Mrs. Cooke gave them all a big smile. "It's time to take my surprise out of the oven," she said.

Katie Lynn gulped. She had eaten some of her mother's surprises before. She could never figure out what they were.

"What is it, Mrs. Cooke?" asked Tina.

"Quiche Lorraine!" said Mrs. Cooke.

"Keesh lo rain?" said Katie Lynn. "What's that?"

"It's a pie filled with eggs, bacon, cream, and cheese all mixed together," replied Mrs. Cooke.

Tina leaned over to Katie Lynn. "I thought pies were supposed to have apples or blueberries in them," she whispered.

"They are," said Katie Lynn. "With ice cream on top!"

But Mrs. Cooke wasn't listening. "I've been watching the French Chef on television," she said. "He says that anyone can be a great French cook."

Katie Lynn wondered if the French Chef had ever tried her mother's cooking.

Mrs. Cooke put on a pair of huge oven mitts and took two round pie tins out of the oven. Something yellow was bubbling over their sides.

"Don't they look wonderful?" Mrs. Cooke said proudly.

"Oh, yes!" said Mr. Cooke and Grandma.

Katie Lynn didn't think they looked wonderful. She thought they looked awful.

"I need to go home," Tina whispered.

"No way!" Katie Lynn whispered back.

Mrs. Cooke began walking slowly toward the table. She was trying to balance a pie tin in each hand.

All of a sudden, one of the tins started to wobble. Mrs. Cooke tried to balance it. She moved to the right, then to the left, then back to the right.

"Why is she dancing?" Tina whispered.

Katie Lynn shrugged. "Maybe you're supposed to dance when you cook French food," she whispered back.

The pie tins continued to wobble, and Mrs. Cooke continued to dance from side to side. One tin started to fall. Mrs. Cooke flung up her arms, sending both tins soaring into the air.

Mrs. Cooke screamed.

Mr. Cooke dived under the table.

"I'm out of here!" cried Tina. She jumped up and ran out of the kitchen.

Katie Lynn was too stunned to move. She thought the pie tins looked like flying saucers.

One landed on the floor with a big *splat*. Then the other landed in the middle of the table with a huge *sploosh*.

Mrs. Cooke looked as if she was going to cry.

But Grandma quickly grabbed a fork. She scraped up some of the quiche from the middle of the table and ate it. "Delicious!" she said.

Mr. Cooke climbed out from under the table. He ate some of the quiche, too. "It has an interesting flavor," he added. Katie Lynn knew he always said that about her mother's cooking.

Now everyone was looking at her. It was her turn to say something, so she picked up her fork and tasted the quiche.

"Uh…that was really good, Mom," she said. Then she gulped down her water.

"Why, thank you, Katie Lynn," said Mrs. Cooke. She gave her a wink. "I guess you and Grandma aren't the only good cooks in this family."

Grandma and Katie Lynn looked at each other. They didn't say anything.

Mr. Cooke just took another bite of quiche.

After dinner, Mrs. Cooke stood up and sighed contentedly. "I am so thrilled that everyone loved my quiche. I can hardly wait to see what the French Chef cooks tomorrow."

Chapter Two

The Goofy French Chef

The next day after school, Katie Lynn and Tina and Grandma were in the kitchen baking their famous Oatmeal Walnut Chocolate Chunk Cookies for the Katie Lynn Cookie Company. Mr. Chesterfield would need his cookie delivery soon for his restaurant. They were almost done, but Tina's little brother, Gerald, kept trying to steal the cookies.

Right now, Gerald was sitting on the floor. He was licking cookie dough off a wooden spoon.

Mrs. Cooke came to the kitchen door.

"*Bonjour,* everyone!" she said. "Katie Lynn, my cooking show is on television. I thought you and I could watch it. Maybe the French Chef will have a new recipe that we can make together."

Katie Lynn turned to Grandma. "Can you and Tina double up while I'm gone?" she asked.

"Certainly, dear, if you take Gerald with you!" said Grandma.

Katie Lynn and Gerald followed Mrs. Cooke back into the living room. The French Chef's face filled the television screen. He had a big droopy mustache and was wearing a tall chef's hat.

Mrs. Cooke beamed at the TV. "Isn't he wonderful?" she asked.

"I think he looks goofy," Gerald said.

Katie Lynn silently agreed.

"Zee secret to good cooking eez using your imagination," said the French Chef. "Today, we are going to cook snails."

Katie Lynn gasped. "Did he say snails?"

"Yes," said Mrs. Cooke. She had a dreamy look on her face. "The French eat a lot of snails."

Suddenly, Katie Lynn's stomach felt funny.

The television camera zoomed in on the snails. They were climbing up the sides of a big glass bowl. Katie Lynn was sure they were trying to escape.

"Oh, wow!" Gerald said. "This is neat!" He was staring at the TV with bug eyes. But Katie Lynn closed hers. She couldn't watch anymore.

Finally, Mrs. Cooke said, "That's what we're going to eat tonight!"

Katie Lynn opened her eyes. *What?* she said.

"Snails," said Mrs. Cooke.

Mrs. Cooke left for the market, and Katie Lynn went back to the kitchen.

She didn't feel so good.

"Well, what are we having for dinner?" asked Grandma.

"Snails," Katie Lynn replied weakly.

"Oh, no!" Grandma gasped.

"Oh, yes," said Katie Lynn. "Mom's gone to the market to get them."

Watch Out for Snails!

Katie Lynn ate some cookies to take her mind off the snails. Then she went back to baking with Grandma and Tina. Gerald was still in the living room, watching reruns of *The French Chef*.

Finally, Katie Lynn said, "We only need one more batch and Mr. Chesterfield's cookies will be ready."

Just then, Mrs. Cooke burst into the kitchen. "I'm back!" she announced. She held up a paper bag. "They had some *wonderful* snails at the market!"

"They're alive!" screamed Tina.

"Of course they're alive, Tina," said Mrs. Cooke. "They're *supposed* to be alive."

"Mom!" cried Katie Lynn. "Some of them are crawling on your dress!"

Mrs. Cooke looked down. "Oh, my goodness! You're right. How in the world did they get out?" She plucked the snails off her dress and put them back inside the paper bag.

Katie Lynn shivered. She hoped no snails ever crawled on *her* clothes!

Mrs. Cooke took a big bowl out of the cupboard and dumped the snails into it.

The snails started crawling up the sides.

They're trying to escape, Katie Lynn thought, *just like the ones on television*.

Katie Lynn went back to mixing together the cookie ingredients while Mrs. Cooke got the snails ready to cook.

Suddenly, Tina screamed, "There's a snail in my cookie dough!"

Katie Lynn looked at Tina's dough. "No, there isn't, Tina. That's just a chocolate chunk."

"But there are some on the floor," said Grandma. "Be careful not to step on them."

Tina started jumping up and down. "I don't want them crawling on me!" she screamed.

"Stop it, Tina!" shouted Katie Lynn. "You just squashed two of them!"

"Oh! Oh! My new shoes!" cried Tina. Now she was hopping around even more. "They're ruined! They're ruined!"

Mrs. Cooke reached down and picked up the snails that hadn't been squashed. She washed them off and put them in a skillet. "That should solve the problem," she said.

"I can't watch this," Tina whispered to Katie Lynn.

"Me neither," said Katie Lynn.

They dropped their cookie dough onto the cookie sheets and put them into the oven. They tried not to look at the skillet with the snails in it.

When the cookies were done, Katie Lynn and Tina took them out of the oven.

"I hope you girls checked your cookie dough carefully," said Mrs. Cooke. "I think some of the snails are missing."

Katie Lynn and Tina looked at each other in horror.

Chapter 4

Frogs' Legs for Dinner

The next morning, Katie Lynn was double-checking the last batch of cookies for snails when the telephone rang.

"Katie Lynn, *ma chérie!* Please answer that!" called Mrs. Cooke. "I'm watching the French Chef and I don't want to be disturbed!"

Katie Lynn grabbed the receiver. "Hello!" she said.

It was Mr. Chesterfield.

"We just ran out of cookies!" he said.

"Don't worry, Mr. Chesterfield. Grandma's on her way with the first half of the order," Katie Lynn said. "We'll deliver the rest of them as soon as possible."

"Great!" said Mr. Chesterfield. He paused. "Have you ever thought about baking other kinds of cookies?" he asked.

"No, not really," said Katie Lynn. "Why?"

"I'm in charge of the Zoo Benefit this year," said Mr. Chesterfield. "And I want to auction off some special cookies to raise money for a new Ape House."

"A new Ape House!" Katie Lynn cried. "That's a great idea!" Katie Lynn thought the animals in the zoo sometimes looked a little sad. She wished they could do something like this for all of them.

"I think so, too, Katie Lynn," said Mr.

Chesterfield. "They need a home that feels more like a jungle."

"Well, I'm sure we can figure out something that will work," said Katie Lynn.

"Good. Let's talk about it later," said Mr. Chesterfield. "Your grandmother just arrived with the cookies."

Mrs. Cooke came into the kitchen as Katie Lynn hung up the receiver. "We're having frogs' legs tonight!" she announced. "The French Chef showed me how to cook them."

"Frogs' legs?" Katie Lynn said.

Mrs. Cooke nodded. "Yes. The French Chef says their flavor leaps right out of the frying pan. He's a food genius!"

Katie Lynn pictured frogs' legs leaping all over their kitchen floor. She tried to think about the new cookie. But all she could think about was cookies with frogs' legs sticking out of them.

She ran next door to Tina's house. Tina was sitting on her front porch, watching Gerald dig in the dirt.

Katie Lynn told her about Mr. Chesterfield's telephone call.

"What kind of cookies would be special?" Tina asked.

Katie Lynn shrugged. "That's what we have to figure out."

"Well, let's not add any chocolate chunks to them," said Tina. "You can't tell those from snails."

"We don't have to worry about snails anymore," said Katie Lynn. "Now it's frogs' legs."

"*Frogs' legs?*" Tina exclaimed.

Katie Lynn nodded. "That's French

cooking, too. Mom went to the market to buy some."

"I thought frogs were pets," said Tina. She looked next door to where Jonathan Wilbarger was sitting on his front porch. He looked upset. "Hey, Jonathan!" she shouted. "Don't you have a pet frog?"

"I used to," Jonathan said sadly. "But Burt disappeared this morning." He sniffled. "I really miss him."

"Katie Lynn's family is eating frogs' legs for dinner tonight," Tina said.

Jonathan's eyes went wide. He jumped up and ran inside his house.

"Why did you tell him that?" demanded Katie Lynn.

Tina shrugged. "It just came out."

"Well, I don't want to talk about frogs anymore. I want to talk about our new cookie," said Katie Lynn. "Come on.

Grandma should be home by now. Maybe she'll have some ideas."

"I can't leave. I'm baby-sitting Gerald," Tina said. "It's my job to make sure he doesn't eat Dad's newspaper."

Katie Lynn rolled her eyes. "Your little brother is so weird."

"I know," said Tina.

Katie Lynn laughed. "Well, bring him with you. Our kitchen can't get any weirder!"

"Okay," said Tina.

She grabbed Gerald's hand, and the three of them ran to Katie Lynn's house. They went straight to the kitchen. Mrs. Cooke was cooking frogs' legs.

Katie Lynn suddenly wondered if Burt's legs were among them.

Chapter 5

Where's Burt?

Katie Lynn told Grandma about the new cookie that Mr. Chesterfield wanted.

"It's very important to the apes, Grandma," she added.

So Grandma got out her recipes. But nothing looked special to them. Some were too hard. Some were too plain. And some had stuff in them that Gerald was allergic to.

"He'll want to lick the spoons," said

25

Tina. "And then he'll start itching all over."

"Ooh la la!" said Mrs. Cooke. "The French Chef was right. These frogs' legs look delicious."

"See you later, Katie Lynn," said Tina.

"You and Gerald are both welcome to stay for dinner, Tina," said Mrs. Cooke.

"Thank you, Mrs. Cooke, but we have to go home," said Tina. "My mother says I eat over here too much."

"You can't leave now," whispered Katie Lynn. "We still haven't decided on a new kind of cookie."

"Sorry," Tina said. "Come on, Gerald."

"Ribbet! Ribbet!" croaked Gerald. He hopped through the door behind her.

Katie Lynn and Grandma set the table.

Mr. Cooke came into the kitchen. He looked nervous.

Mrs. Cooke put a huge platter in the center of the table. "Ta-da!" she said. "Frogs' legs! *Bon appétit!*"

Just then, the front doorbell rang.

"I'll get it!" said Mr. Cooke. He jumped up from the table and ran out of the room.

Dad's never coming back tonight, Katie Lynn thought. *He won't have to eat frogs' legs like the rest of us.*

All of a sudden, Mr. Cooke reappeared at the door to the kitchen. Jonathan Wilbarger was right behind him. Jonathan looked as if he had been crying.

"Where's Burt?" Jonathan demanded. He was looking at the huge platter of frogs' legs on the table.

"I don't know what you're talking about, Jonathan," said Mr. Cooke.

"Those are his legs!" Jonathan cried. He

pointed to two of the biggest legs on the platter. "That's what's left of Burt!" He looked at Mrs. Cooke. "I can't believe you cooked my pet frog! Burt was part of our family."

"But I bought these frogs' legs at the market," said Mrs. Cooke.

Jonathan walked over to the table and took the two big frogs' legs off the platter. "Don't worry, Burt," he said. "I don't know where the rest of you is, but I'll always take care of your legs."

Then he turned and left the kitchen.

Katie Lynn heard the front door slam.

For several minutes, no one said anything.

Then Mrs. Cooke stood up. "I'm not hungry anymore," she said. She left the kitchen.

Grandma followed her out.

Katie Lynn looked at her father. "Now what do we do?" she asked.

"Come on. Let's go to Burger-Rama," Mr. Cooke whispered. "We can pick up Tina and deliver the rest of Mr. Chesterfield's cookies on the way home."

"Great idea, Dad!" Katie Lynn whispered back. She ran to the telephone and called Tina.

"Is it okay if Gerald comes with us?" Tina asked.

"Sure," said Katie Lynn. "Dad's already read his newspaper today."

Animal Cookies

Katie Lynn, Tina, and Gerald hurried into Chesterfield's Restaurant.

Mr. Chesterfield was standing at the cash register.

"Here are the rest of your cookies, Mr. Chesterfield," said Katie Lynn.

"We checked them all for snails," Tina added. "We didn't find any."

Mr. Chesterfield gasped. *"Snails?* What? There are *snails* in my cookies?"

"No! No!" Katie Lynn said. She gave Tina a dirty look. Suddenly, she remembered what the French Chef had said about using your imagination. "We're, uh...baking animal cookies for the Zoo Benefit. Isn't that exciting?"

"I don't want any animals in my cookies!" Mr. Chesterfield cried.

Tina and Gerald giggled.

"We're not going to put animals *in* the cookies, Mr. Chesterfield! They'll just be *shaped* like animals!" said Katie Lynn.

"Oh," said Mr. Chesterfield. "A cookie zoo! I get it! I love it!"

Katie Lynn and Tina grinned at each other.

"But the Zoo Benefit is Sunday afternoon, girls. And everybody in town is invited. So I'll need lots and lots of animal cookies," said Mr. Chesterfield. "Do you think you can have them ready by then?"

"No problem," said Katie Lynn. "We'll bake them tomorrow."

When they got back home, Katie Lynn told Grandma about the animal cookies.

"We can use my regular sugar cookie recipe," said Grandma. "It'll be perfect."

"And we can twist the dough into all kinds of animal shapes," said Katie Lynn.

"And we can use chocolate chips for the eyes and mouths," said Tina.

"We can put different-colored icing on them, too," Grandma suggested.

"Goody! Goody!" Gerald cried.

Grandma got out the icing recipe and put it on the counter.

"Tomorrow's Saturday," said Katie Lynn. "We'll start baking bright and early so the cookies will be ready in time for the benefit on Sunday."

When Katie Lynn got up the next morning, Tina and Gerald were in the kitchen with Grandma. Grandma had heated the oven to 400° Fahrenheit.

Katie Lynn and Tina gathered the ingredients for the new cookie:

3/4 CUP SHORTENING

1 CUP SUGAR

2 EGGS

1 TEASPOON VANILLA

2 1/2 CUPS ALL-PURPOSE FLOUR
    (NOT SELF-RISING)

1 TEASPOON BAKING POWDER

1 TEASPOON SALT

They thoroughly mixed the shortening, the sugar, the eggs, and the vanilla by hand.

Then they gradually added the flour, the baking powder, and the salt, and kept mixing until everything was blended.

They covered the dough with a dish

towel and put it in the refrigerator to chill.

After an hour, they used their hands to roll some of the dough into coils. They wound the coils up to look like snails.

Then they added chocolate chips for eyes.

To make a rabbit, they rolled out some of the dough with a rolling pin. Then they cut out two circles with the mouth of a drinking glass. They used one circle for a rabbit's head. They cut the other circle in half. They shaped the halves to make the rabbit's ears. They rolled up little pieces of leftover dough to make the whiskers. They added chocolate chips for the eyes and nose.

Then they rolled up some of the dough into small balls. They flattened each ball slightly to make a frog's body. They took some of the leftover coils from the snails and bent them to make frog legs. They made smaller balls of dough, put chocolate chips in them, and stuck them on for eyes.

They made chocolate chip mouths.

They made as many kinds of animals as they could think of.

Then they put the animals on an ungreased baking sheet and baked them until they were golden brown—between seven and ten minutes.

After they finished several batches, Grandma said, "We'll cover them with wax paper, and we can put the icing on them tomorrow."

Katie Lynn and Tina gave each other a high-five.

"We did it!" Katie Lynn cried. "The cookies are almost ready, and now nothing can go wrong!"

Chapter 7

This Place Is a Zoo!

On Sunday morning, Katie Lynn tried to watch the French Chef with her mother. But her mother kept asking Katie Lynn to French-braid her hair.

"I think I'll be a better French cook if I look more French," her mother said. "Don't you?"

"It might help, Mom," said Katie Lynn.

When a commercial came on, she snuck

into the kitchen. Grandma and Tina and Gerald were sitting at the table.

"It looks like we're safe for today," she said. "The French Chef hasn't said anything about snails or frogs' legs."

"Thank goodness," said Tina. She bit off the ear of a rabbit cookie. "I don't think I could stand any more animals in this kitchen."

Katie Lynn sat down with them. "Have you made the icing yet?" she asked.

Grandma and Tina just looked at each other.

"*Zut alors!*" said Gerald. He laughed. "*Zut alors!*"

"What's Gerald saying?" asked Katie Lynn.

"He's saying, 'Oh, no!' in French," explained Grandma.

"We think he's picking it up from the French Chef," said Tina.

"Why's he saying, 'Oh, no!'?" asked Katie Lynn.

"We can't find the icing recipe," Grandma said.

"What?" Katie Lynn cried.

"We think Gerald ate it," added Tina.

Katie Lynn gasped. "Oh, no! Do you remember what was in it, Grandma?"

"Just bits and pieces," said Grandma. "But Tina and I have tried all kinds of combinations, and nothing works. At least, according to Gerald."

"Gerald!" Katie Lynn said. "What do you mean?"

"We let him taste each new icing," Tina explained. "If he spits it out, then it isn't any good." With a sigh, she added, "So far, he's spit out everything we've given him."

Gerald laughed. *"Zut alors! Zut alors!"* he said again.

"Zut alors is right," said Katie Lynn. "I can't believe the new Ape House depends on Gerald. What does he know? He's the reason we're in this mess."

"He knows cookie icings," said Tina.

"Well, we'll just have to keep trying," said Katie Lynn. "The Zoo Benefit is this afternoon."

Just then, Mrs. Cooke came into the kitchen. "The French Chef showed us how to make a very simple sauce," she announced. "That's what we're going to have for dinner tonight."

"That's wonderful, Kathy," Grandma said. She sounded tired. "What are we going to put it on?"

Mrs. Cooke got a puzzled look on her face. "We're not going to put it on anything, Mother. We're going to eat it like a soup."

Tina made a gagging sound.

Katie Lynn bit her lip to keep from giggling.

"Well, that's nice, dear," Grandma said. "I'm sure it'll be an interesting experience for all of us."

"*Oui! Oui! Oui!*" said Mrs. Cooke in her best French accent. She grinned. "The French Chef always says that to people."

While Mrs. Cooke made her sauce, Katie Lynn, Grandma, and Tina kept trying to make a cookie icing.

"Please like this, Gerald," said Katie Lynn. She gave him a bite of icing number ten.

"Yech!" said Gerald. He stuck out his tongue at them.

Suddenly, Mrs. Cooke sighed.

"What's wrong, Mom?" Katie Lynn asked.

"This just doesn't taste like a sauce," Mrs. Cooke said. "I don't know what happened."

"Well, don't worry about it, Mom," said Katie Lynn. She gave her mother a big hug.

"I don't know where I went wrong," Mrs. Cooke said. "I must have misunderstood the French Chef's accent."

"Stop that, Gerald!" Tina cried.

Everyone turned to look at Gerald. He was licking his fingers.

"What's he doing?" asked Katie Lynn.

"He's eating your mother's sauce!" said Tina.

Suddenly, Katie Lynn gasped. "But look at him! He didn't spit it out!"

Katie Lynn stuck her finger in the mixing bowl. She scooped out some of her mother's sauce and then licked it off. She was absolutely amazed. The sauce was delicious.

"This is it! This is it!" she cried. "This is the icing we need!"

"It's not an icing, Katie Lynn," said Mrs. Cooke. "It's a sauce."

"I don't care, Mom! It's wonderful," said Katie Lynn. "You've done what we couldn't do. You've come up with an icing we can put on our animal cookies."

"But what about dinner tonight?" Mrs. Cooke said.

"Don't worry about that, Mom," said Katie Lynn. "If you can show us how to make this, dinner tonight will be on the Katie Lynn Cookie Company."

Grandma tasted the sauce and cried, "Oh, Kathy! Katie Lynn's right! This is incredible!"

"What's in it, Mrs. Cooke?" asked Tina.

Mrs. Cooke got a funny look on her face. "I'm not sure," she said.

The Secret's in the Sauce

Katie Lynn looked at the kitchen clock. There were only a couple of hours before the Zoo Benefit.

"What do you mean, Mom?" she said.

"I didn't write down the recipe," said Mrs. Cooke. "It was so simple, I didn't think I'd forget the ingredients."

"Do you remember any of them?" asked Tina.

"Well, sort of," said Mrs. Cooke.

"Then let's just mix those together," said Grandma.

"But I also added other things," said Mrs. Cooke.

"Why?" asked Katie Lynn.

"It wasn't looking like the sauce on television. But then I remembered something the French Chef always says," said Mrs. Cooke. *"All good cooks add their own personal touches."*

"So what was your personal touch?" asked Tina.

"I don't remember," said Mrs. Cooke.

"Oh, this is terrible!" said Katie Lynn. "We have the perfect icing for our animal cookies, and we don't even know what's in it."

"Well, we just all need to relax and take

this one step at a time," said Grandma.

Everyone took a deep breath and sat down at the kitchen table.

"I think the first thing I put in the bowl was flour," Mrs. Cooke finally said. She pointed to a blue canister on the counter. "I got it out of that."

"Oh!" said Katie Lynn. "That's powdered sugar!"

"How much did you use?" asked Grandma.

"Three cups," said Mrs. Cooke. "I sifted it first."

Katie Lynn wrote down what her mother said.

"What next?" asked Grandma.

Slowly but surely, Mrs. Cooke remembered what she had put in the mixing bowl.

In addition to three cups of sifted powdered sugar, she used:

6 TABLESPOONS SOFTENED BUTTER

4 TABLESPOONS MILK

1/4 TEASPOON PEPPERMINT EXTRACT
(which Mrs. Cooke thought was vinegar)

4 DROPS RED FOOD COLORING (which
Mrs. Cooke thought was beet juice)

Grandma looked over at Katie Lynn.
"Did you get all that?"

Katie Lynn nodded.

When they were sure they had all the
ingredients Mrs. Cooke used, they mixed
some of the "sauce" by hand.

"It tastes just like Mom's!" cried Katie
Lynn. "We have the icing for the new
cookie! Now all we have to do is mix up
different colors for the different animals."

She gave her mother a big hug and added, "You've saved the Katie Lynn Cookie Company."

"Come on, girls! There's no time to waste!" said Grandma. "Let's get started."

They made blue icing for the snails.

They made green icing for the frogs.

They made white icing for the rabbits.

They made other colors for other animals.

Soon, all the animal cookies looked like real animals.

Finally, they were finished.

"Do you think Mr. Chesterfield will like them?" asked Katie Lynn.

"Well, there's only one way to find out," said Grandma. "Let's take these cookies to the Zoo Benefit!"

Chapter 9

Everyone Goes Ape!

Everyone piled into the car, and Mr. Cooke drove to the zoo.

Tina gasped. "Where'd all these people come from?" she said.

"Mr. Chesterfield said everyone in town would be at the Zoo Benefit," said Katie Lynn. "He was right."

"I'm sure they all came to buy your animal cookies," Mr. Cooke said.

He grinned at Katie Lynn and Tina.

"I hope so," said Katie Lynn. "We want to make enough money to build a new Ape House."

Gerald made ape noises in the back seat.

"We need to hurry. Mr. Chesterfield is probably wondering where we are," Grandma said. "Everyone grab a container of cookies."

They rushed to the main entrance. Mr. Chesterfield was waiting for them.

"There you are!" he said. He got a big smile on his face when Katie Lynn showed him the animal cookies. "Perfect! Perfect! I knew I could count on the Katie Lynn Cookie Company!"

"Of course!" said Katie Lynn.

She and Tina grinned at each other.

Then they all followed Mr. Chesterfield to a big blue tent. On the way, they passed the apes.

"It won't be long now," Katie Lynn shouted to them. "You'll soon have a new home!"

Jonathan Wilbarger ran up to them. He had a frog in his hands. "I found Burt. He

was in our backyard the whole time." He looked at Mrs. Cooke. "I'm sorry I said you fried his legs."

"That's okay, Jonathan," said Mrs. Cooke. "I'm just glad you found him."

Katie Lynn and Tina put the animal cookies on big silver trays. Then Mr. Chesterfield auctioned them off. Jonathan

Wilbarger bought a whole batch of frog cookies. He even gave one to Gerald for a pet. Within minutes, the cookies were all gone.

"What a success!" Mr. Chesterfield exclaimed. "We made a lot of money for the new Ape House."

Katie Lynn thought it was a success, too. "Three cheers for Mom and her French cooking!"

"Thanks, but I've decided to give that up," said Mrs. Cooke. "I've learned all the French Chef has to teach."

Katie Lynn looked at Grandma and Mr. Cooke. She was sure they were thinking the same thing. *What a relief!*

"Really?" said Tina.

"Yes," said Mrs. Cooke. "Tonight I'm watching a show about Italian cooking. Tomorrow we're going to have octopus for dinner." She kissed the tips of her fingers. *"Delizioso!"*

Katie Lynn almost choked on the cookie she was eating. Then she laughed. "Okay, Mom," she said. "And we'll make octopus cookies for dessert!"

To make Katie Lynn's octopus cookies:

Roll out sugar cookie dough on a floured board or counter.

Cut out circles with the mouth of a drinking glass to make the body of the octopuses.

Put some flour on your hands to keep dough from sticking. Roll some of the left-over dough between your hands to make the tentacles.

Attach four or five tentacles to the bottom of each circle.

Use chocolate chips for the eyes and mouth.

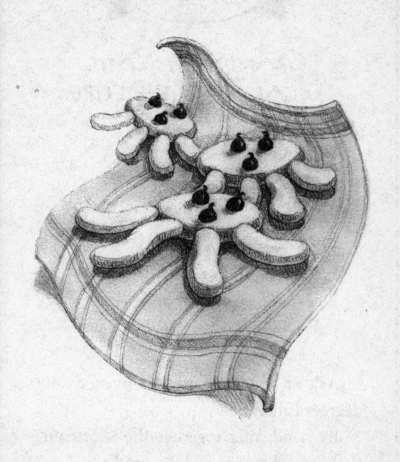

GRANDMA'S BASIC SUGAR COOKIE RECIPE

3/4 CUP SHORTENING

1 CUP SUGAR

2 EGGS

1 TEASPOON VANILLA

2 1/2 CUPS ALL-PURPOSE FLOUR
    (NOT SELF-RISING)

1 TEASPOON BAKING POWDER

1 TEASPOON SALT

Ask an adult to preheat oven to 400 degrees Fahrenheit.

By hand, mix together the shortening, the sugar, the eggs, and the vanilla.

Then gradually add the flour, the baking powder, and the salt and keep mixing until it's all blended.

Cover the dough with a dish towel and put it in the refrigerator to chill for one hour.

Roll it out on a floured board or counter. Use the mouth of a glass to cut out regular sugar cookies. Or use your hands to make them into animal shapes.

Put the cookies on an ungreased baking sheet. Ask an adult to put the baking sheet into the oven.

Bake the cookies for 7 to 10 minutes, or until they are golden brown.

Ask an adult to take the baking sheet out of the oven.

Let cookies cool before icing.

Mrs. Cooke's Cookie "Sauce" Recipe

3 CUPS SIFTED POWDERED SUGAR

6 TABLESPOONS SOFTENED BUTTER

4 TABLESPOONS MILK

1/4 TEASPOON PEPPERMINT EXTRACT

4 DROPS (MORE OR LESS) OF FOOD COLORING

Mix by hand until thoroughly blended.

The Battle of the Bakers has begun!

Can the Katie Lynn Cookie Company stand the heat? Find out in

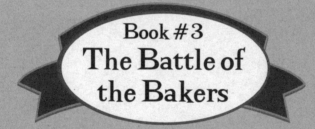

Book #3
**The Battle of
the Bakers**

Victory has never tasted so sweet...

ABOUT THE AUTHOR

G. E. STANLEY is the author of more than fifty books for young people, many of them award winners. He and his wife, Gwen, live in Lawton, Oklahoma. They have two sons, Charles and James, a daughter-in-law, Tambye, and a family dog, a Labrador retriever named Daisy.

"I've always loved to bake cookies. But I remember one summer when I was a kid, I had to share our kitchen with my mother and my grandmother, just as Katie Lynn does in *Frogs' Legs for Dinner?*" says G. E. Stanley. "My grandmother, who even then was getting more and more confused about things, liked to fry her chicken in a very thick batter. Unfortunately, one evening, she mistook my cookie dough for her chicken batter, so we ended up having cookie-dough fried chicken!"

ABOUT THE ILLUSTRATOR

LINDA DOCKEY GRAVES was born in Eureka, California, and grew up in the Berkshires, in Massachusetts. She now lives with her family and pets in Chesapeake, Virginia. This is the San Jose State University graduate's twenty-second children's book. When not illustrating children's books, Linda loves baking, eating, and sharing hot, soft chocolate chip cookies with her family and friends.